My 1st Classic Story

Paul Bunyan

a retelling by Eric Blair

illustrated by Micah Chambers-Goldberg

PICTURE WINDOW BOOKS

a capstone imprint

My First Classic Story is published by Picture Window Books
A Capstone Imprint
151 Good Counsel Drive, P.O. Box 669
Mankato, Minnesota 56002
www.capstonepub.com

Library of Congress Cataloging-in-Publication data
is available on the library of congress website.
ISBN: 978-1-4048-6580-8 (library binding)

Summary: A retelling of the classic tale of Paul Bunyan.

Art Director: Kay Fraser
Graphic Designer: Emily Harris
Production Specialist: Michelle Biedscheid

For generations, storytelling was
the main form of entertainment.
Some of the greatest stories were tall
tales, or exaggerated stories that may
or may not have been about real people.

Many people believe that the tale of
Paul Bunyan started in logging camps
in the 1800s. The following retelling
revisits some of the most famous
Paul Bunyan adventures.

Paul Bunyan was a big boy. When he was born, it took six giant storks to deliver him.

His first baby carriage was a lumber wagon pulled by oxen.

He ate forty bowls of oatmeal for breakfast.

Soon, Paul grew so large that his mom had to sew his pants from blankets. His shirts were made from tents.

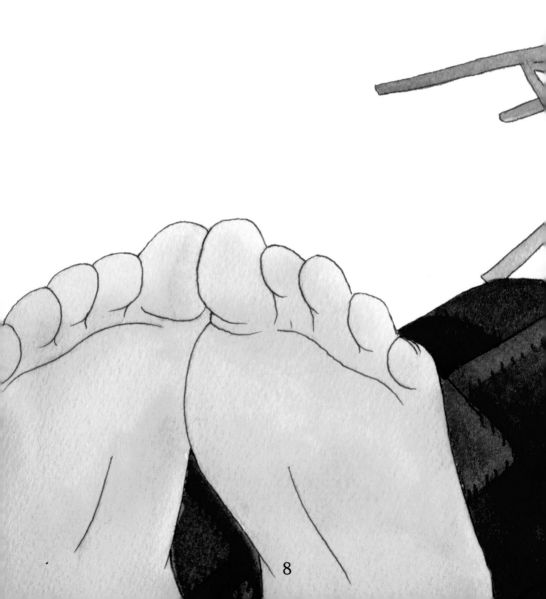

Before long, Paul grew taller than the trees.
He was stronger than any man alive.

Paul was too big to sleep in the house.
Instead, he slept in the barn.

Paul and his parents lived in the Great North Woods.

Sometimes, the weather was so cold that the snow and ice turned blue.

One day, Paul saw a pair of blue eyes in a large snowdrift.

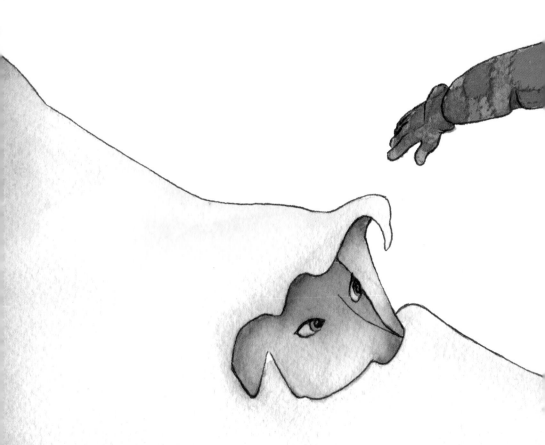

When Paul dug into the snow, he found
a blue baby ox. The ox was frozen solid.

Paul blew on the baby ox. His giant breath brought the ox back to life.

Babe the Blue Ox became Paul's best friend.
Babe grew to be as big as Paul.

Since Paul lived in the Great North Woods,
he decided to become a lumberjack.

Paul became the best lumberjack in the world. He could cut down ten trees with just one swing of his huge ax.

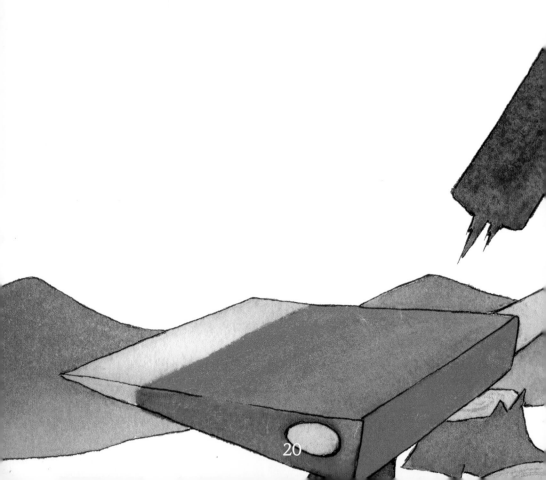

Paul and Babe joined a logging team.
They taught the loggers to make giant pancakes.
They used shovels to turn the pancakes.

But Paul and Babe missed traveling.

After a while, Paul and Babe left the loggers.

The two friends started a new trip to the West.

When it rained, the tracks made by Paul's and Babe's feet filled with water. The tracks became the Great Lakes.

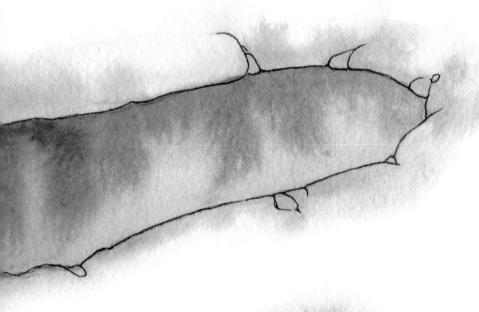

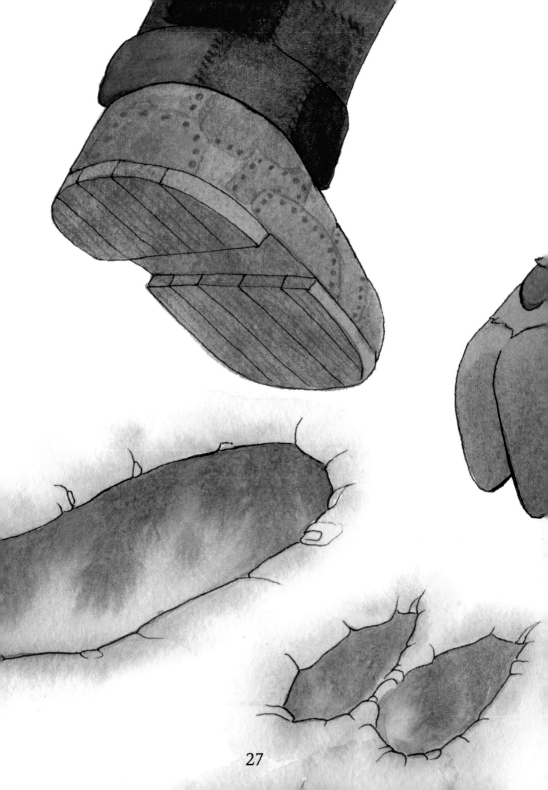

Along the way, Paul and Babe cleared so much forest that the West became treeless.

People called this land the Great Plains.

Paul and Babe missed all the trees.
They decided to return to the Great
North Woods.

And that's where they still live today.